THE KITTERY KID

The Kittery Kid by Yarp N. Derf
originally published in 1959

This edition ©2014 by RiverRun Select
A project of Piscataqua Press and
RiverRun Bookstore
142 Fleet Street | Portsmouth, NH |
03801

www.piscataquapress.com
www.riverrunbookstore.com

ISBN: 978-1-939739-45-2

Printed in the United States of America

Cover art: Ken Fellows

THE KITTERY KID

A True Story, Mind you

By

YARP N. DERF

EXCERPTED

By

KRISTIN AND KEN FELLOWS

FORWARD

The original book, *The Kittery Kid*, was a 145 page rambling, coming-of-age memoir of the boyhood and early manhood of "Yarp N. Derf ." This pseudonymous author (Fred N. Pray) actually was the Kittery Kid and lived the life of calamity, pleasure, humor and trouble he detailed in the original version.

The Kittery Kid was published by Vantage Press Inc., 120 West 31st St., New York 1, N.Y. in 1959. From information in the original book, Fred Pray would have been in his 6th or 7th decade at that time. The period of time covered in The Kittery Kid itself, would have been approximately 1890 to 1920. Although the book is primarily an entertaining one, especially for children, the Kittery/Portsmouth landmarks described, the local roads, buildings, businesses and waterways mentioned, and the local characters named make the Kittery Kid interesting for adults and a fascinating historical reference as well.

ABOUT THE AUTHOR

Yarp N. Derf (Fred Pray) was born in Kittery, Maine, lived for many years in Portsmouth, New Hampshire, and (made) his home in Sanford, Maine (probably when the book was written). Hunting, fishing, and wood-working, all of which he learned as a boy, as described in The Kittery Kid, (were) his hobbies. The Kittery Kid (was) his first book.

Portsmouth

Piscacataqua

Kittery Foreside

Portsmouth Naval Shipyard

Back Channel

Whipple Rd

①

③

236

Woodlawn Ave ("the Avenue")

④

②

Whipple Rd

(103)

Admiralty Village

Spruce Creek

Kittery Point

① "House on the River"
② "Home on "the Avenue""
③ Lock's Cove
④ Austin School

THE HOUSE
ON THE RIVER

I was born in Kittery in the Skipper Billie House at the lower end of foreside. (I never knew what side this was or what it was a side of, so we will skip it).

The house was on the bank of the river known as the Back Channel and set back about fifty feet from the high-water mark with a steep slope to the shore line.

I had five sisters older than I. The one next to me was three years older and was my playmate. Of course, I played some with Zeek, my brother who was eighteen months younger, because I was supposed to look after him more or less – and it was mostly less.

The older sister was the acting mother when Mother was busy with other things; and with such a large family, there were a lot of other things.

Father was a good provider. He did all the buying and paying. He would buy wholesale in large quantities, for it took large amounts to feed all of us. You see, there were ten of us, including the hired girl. I have seen wagon loads come to the house with a quarter of beef, a whole dressed lamb, half a pig, a quintal of salt fish, barrel of flour and sugar, kerosene oil, crackers—pilot and broken, a large firkin of salt mackerel, lard, and a half-barrel of molasses.

There was a good-sized barn and a shed that had a loft. The ground floor was stocked with wood, corn for hens, garden tools and such.

I can see it now, the thick salt fish hanging by the tail where we could strip off a piece any time to eat, and skates' fins dried and hanging by string. The fins dried quickly and were nice when used for fish cakes. The loft was a woodworking and paint shop.

We kept a cow in the barn and chickens under it; and we always planted a large garden, for Father always rented a place where the land would help him pay the rent, by working it for vegetables and hay. My sisters helped in the garden and at hay time. From the garden we always had plenty of good food and vegetables, and with Mother cooking them, they were sure good to eat.

The hen-feed was whole yellow corn and was kept in a large hinged covered box. Zeek and I on hot summer days would take off our pants and drawers and bury our lower extremities in the cool corn.

One day our cousin, a young man at this time, had painted Zeek's highchair a dark brown; it was set in the lower part of the shed to dry near the corn box. My back was to the chair and I didn't see Zeek climb into it and sit down. The paint wasn't dry and he got his buttocks smeared with the brown paint. I was frightened because I was supposed to look after him, so I got him down to the shore and told him to drag his bottom on the rocks; he did get some paint off. Then I tried to brush off the paint with seaweed but that stuck to him, so I had to take him to the house where I could get soap and water. The hired girl saw us and told Mother. How she did laugh when she knew what had happened! (Gosh, I was relieved). She got Zeek's bottom nice and clean. The cousin asked if she wanted him to paint the chair again. She said no, for she liked the imprint of Zeek's buttocks.

There was a man named Gus, who had a fish weir at the harbor mouth, and he went by the house in his dory going to Portsmouth to sell his fish. He would stop and ask Father or Mother if they would like some fish and tell them what he had in the dory, and they would tell him what was in the garden he could have in exchange. One day when Father was home Gus stopped by, and the dory was as full of good-sized mackerel as he dared to load it. Father sent me to the shop for a basket. When I got back, Gus was growling, and at first I thought they had disagreed about something and so I listened. He was telling about a horse that had gotten into the weir and torn the netting very badly, or so he described it to Father. The more they talked the more confused I became, and when Gus left and we were walking to the house, I told Father I couldn't see how a horse could get in the weir out in the deep water. He stopped, turned and looked at me, and bust out laughing. He then proceeded to tell me it wasn't a four-legged horse but a horse mackerel, a fish that looks like a mackerel but grows to great size, some weighing as much as nine hundred pounds. This fish is called tuna by the sport fisherman; but by Gus, a damn horse.

Our neighbor, Mrs. Newson, made and sold potato yeast for bread. Mother would send one of us to buy it by the quart. The Newsons were old people and had no children. They were the quietest people I ever saw. When I knocked at the back door, I was asked to sit in the kitchen while Mrs. Newson went to the cellar for the yeast. The only sound was the tick of the old grandfather clock in the corner of the living room. It was such a change from the noise at our house, you felt as if you had to whisper if you wanted to say anything. Now whenever I see or hear a grandfather clock, I always think of the Newsons.

I built a tree house in the balsam tree by the side of the barn. It was close to the Newson's cove. My sister and I used it as a lookout to spy on the neighbors as we thought one of the neighbors was always busy about his house and garden. One in particular used wood all the time, and he would split and pile the wood when other chores were done; it was the neatest woodpile I ever saw, even and straight. Every Saturday he would get in his wherry at the last of the flood tide with his market basket that would hold half a bushel and a wicker demijohn that held a gallon; he would row to Portsmouth for his groceries and fill the jug with rum, and then would row home on the ebb-tide. Some Saturdays he would go forenoons and some afternoons, according to the tide. He would drink that gallon of rum during the week, but I never saw him when I thought he showed the effect of the rum. He was a retired sea captain. There were a lot of men around his age who had followed the sea who always drank rum, just as a lot of farmers had to have their hard cider to drink. The wife died first and he kept the house, and everyone said it was kept neatly. One day he was missed about his yard and they found him dead, sitting in his chair with a Bible in his lap. They had children, one son a very neat, fine man, but the parents were very independent and wanted no help from him.

One day the Ward boys were in a boat and the Emery boy was in the water. They wouldn't let him in the boat. He kept hollering for them to let him in, and that he would drown if they didn't. I began shouting to them to let him into the boat and then I started to cry. Mother came out to see what was the matter, and when I told her she said that he wouldn't drown, that the boys were just having fun. Then (the boys) came ashore at the front of the house and one asked Mother if they could take me sailing. She said yes. The Wards owned a fine sailing yacht. This was the first time I had been in a sailboat. They let me help steer. I had a wonderful time.

Soon after this adventure, we moved from the place to a house on the Avenue near Lock's Cove. When we moved from the Skipper Billie place to the Avenue I was about seven and a half years old.

THE SCHOOL

The school was built on a lot given the town by Reverend James Austin. When the town built the school, he promised to give a bell if a belfry was provided for it.

It was the only school in town that had a bell and was known as the Austin School, Number 7 District. It was on top of a hill and we kids had good sliding down the hill during the winter term. There were two large horse chestnut trees in the yard and we had lots of fun throwing a string with two nuts tied to the end. It would wind around anything if thrown the right way. We liked to wind it around the girl's legs. We also made small baskets by digging out the inside of a nut and cutting away a quarter of each side to form the handle of the basket. These baskets were for the girls of our choice.

We had two ways of admitting a boy in our school. One was for two boys to stand on each side of him and each take the foot and hand on his side. Then they would both swing him between them and bump his bottom against anything that was flat-sided and firm. The other way was to pick a boy of his size to fight him. I know, for once I was chosen. I asked the new boy what his name was. He said John. I asked him where he came from. He said Beverly Farms. I said "Is that so?" and slapped him across the face and we stared at each other. It wasn't long before I was thinking that Beverly Farms boys could fight, and a little while later, I knew they could because he licked the daylights out of me. Believe it or not, we became the best of friends and chummed around together after that.

John's father was a trawl fisherman,

and he would give John his old trawls for us to fish with in the river and harbor.

Our teacher was Miss Crawsby, a beautiful girl. They said she washed her face with milk to keep her complexion. She had no discipline in the school at all; we did anything we wanted to do.

I had a large, long leather pocketbook that I used to catch bumblebees and hornets in. I just had to snap the opening over them. When I got in the schoolroom, I would let the poor things out so they could fly around. Every toad, frog, snake, beetle, or for that matter, anything that could move by itself I thought should be brought to the schoolroom.

I was happy when I found a good-sized turtle. Not only could he move, but he made a scraping sound that I liked. Crabs from the river were quite good, but they didn't move around much. Of course, the girls were frightened by these things and if they weren't, they made out they were. I, sometimes, was frightened. The teacher, poor soul, was frightened and asked the boys to put them out of the schoolroom. We would all volunteer.

We'd start them on the boys' side of the room and chase and prod all the things that would move over to the girls' side. All the girls would be standing on their desks before we got the last live thing out. The girls enjoyed the confusion as much as we boys.

I would catch flies and pull the bristles off a brush and stick the bristles in their hind ends so they would fly around. They looked funny trailing bristles behind. If the fly couldn't take off, I would cut off the bristle until it could fly.

The bell rope hung in the stairwell on the second floor. The janitor had to reach over the stair railing to get it, and of course, the upper end was around the wheel that swung the bell. It also hung through the attic. Three of the boys (I was one of them) fixed a cellar window so it looked as if it was locked but wasn't, and we could get in the school anytime we wished. About every two weeks we would enter the school, take the ladder that hung on the wall of the boys' entry and climb through the trap door into the attic. Then we would climb a flight of steps to the belfry trap door. We would cut the rope so it hung by a small strand just below the point where it left the wheel. When the janitor went to ring the bell, the rope fell down. It would take him at least three-quarters of an hour to fix it. The first time we cut it, he had to climb up in the belfry to ring the bell by hand. We passed the word to the boys we could trust, and told them what we heard about the rope being cut so we three wouldn't be the only boys late to school. We boys had no way of telling time…we had no watches.

After this happened, the janitor screwed an eye-bolt into the wall and with a piece of chain and a padlock secured the ladder to the wall. He bought a cheap lock that was riveted together by three rivets. One night we cut the rivets so we could pry it apart and put it together again. It was a clever job, and you couldn't tell it by looking at it closely. When we did this, we brought all the keys we could find around our homes, but none of them would fit, so the rope was cut again. It was thought we reached the belfry from the outside. We cut the rope three times before they bought a wire rope. Just for fun, we sawed it so it would break once more, and let it go at that.

Another time when it was good skating, John and I (we didn't trust any other boys) went to the belfry using the ladder they thought was secured to the wall. We had two pieces of board and two bricks (we measured the chimney in the cellar to get the size of the boards), carried them the length of the building at least sixty feet by straddling the roof, one foot on each side of the roof (peak). When we reached the chimney I, who had gone first (glad I did), couldn't reach the top of the chimney, so John climbed on my shoulders and I passed the boards and bricks up. It was at night when we did this. I don't think I could have done it if I'd seen how high up we were. I wouldn't do it now for a thousand dollars. We went to school the next morning and were as surprised as the rest to hear there wouldn't be school that day. The janitor had the stovepipe down the length of the room for the benefit of the heat from the pipe since the stove was in front of the room. He had cut a birch tree, trimmed off the branches, and was pushing it in the stovepipe hole. As for the center of the room, it was a mess, all covered with soot. It was two days before they found the boards and bricks. I have often wondered who they got to go to that chimney and find them. I never inquired for I didn't want them to think I was interested, not even in the $75 offered to anyone who could tell them who had placed the boards and bricks over the chimney flue.

I mentioned before that John's father gave him his old trawls. We set them in the rivers, and when the tide was slack—we knew what time that was—we would leave school and haul them in. Miss Crawsby would ask us where we were going, and we would say; "On an errand, and just keep going." As I said, she had no discipline at all. We kids had a fine time that term.

The town officials hired a man teacher the next term. He was a big man and one we boys will never forget. The first morning he told us he was hired to restore order and he was going to have strict discipline in his school. He said he had permission from parents and town officials not to spare the rod.

The first recess, four of the big boys made a plan to gang up and teach him a thing or two. The boys were George, Howard, Frank and Horace. George was to stand up at the blackboard which was near his seat, and when the teacher asked him what he was doing he was to throw an eraser at him. Then when the teacher started toward him, Howard and Frank were to close in behind him, and Horace was to pair up with George.

The plan missed fire (sic), for when Howard and Frank started to leave their seats, the teacher turned on them. Howard was the first; the teacher punched him in the stomach and when he bent over, gave him an upper cut to the jaw. Down he went! Frank swung a right for the teacher's jaw. The teacher ducked and planted his right to Frank's jaw and he went down too. Next, the teacher started for George who ran out of the room. Horace, who was behind the teacher, started for him. Our teacher turned like a flash and punched Horace in the chest so hard he also landed on the floor.

The girls were screaming and the smaller boys, including myself, just stared with our mouths open. He told the girls to be quiet, for everything was all right. He certainly cleaned up that gang! He dragged the boys by the collar and had them sitting up on the floor against the wall. Then he asked one of the Manson boys to get a bucket of water from the boys' room. He dashed the water in their faces. When they came to, he said, "Don't we have fun?" He said he wished there were more of them and said sometime they would all get together out in the school yard and have a real good time; but then he said he might be a little rough, and if any bones were broken it would be their doing, not his! He called for all to go to their seats, said to the three boys not to feel bad, for they couldn't win all the time, especially at a game they didn't know much about; and for the boy who wouldn't stand by as he had agreed, he was sorry and guessed he must be a coward.

That noon all of us boys talked about the scrap and all agreed he was the best teacher we had ever seen. George felt very bad about running out and he showed it for a long time; the other three felt sorry for him. The teacher then said he was going to have discipline even if a few bones were broken and heads cracked. We tried all sorts of petty stuff like scuffing our feet and humming in unison. He let the girls go home and kept us boy after school for an hour. That hurt!

We started to bring bumblebees, hornets, bugs, frogs, toads, or anything that would move into the classroom—just as we had done with the other teacher. Our teacher stopped this almost before it was started. Each morning and noon he would lock the boy's entrance door, let all the girls in and lock their door. Then he let us in. He had placed a table to the side of the door and made all of us boys empty our pockets. No table in the world ever held the variety of things and trash that that table did. He caught me with three bumblebees and a hornet in my long pocketbook and a toad in my coat pocket.

He told me to go to my seat, and he'd deal with me later. He did. I was to dust the erasers, wash the blackboard, and collect small pieces of chalk for two weeks. He always stayed after school, for he had papers to correct and programs for the next day. He claimed he liked company, especially if they made themselves useful.

We didn't like the way he put a stop to our taking things into the schoolroom. We thought he should have warned us what would happen if we didn't stop, about the punishment and the method and quickness of catching us. We knew he was a lot smarter than we were and we didn't like it at all.

John and I were fishing with the trawls in the river, but we didn't leave the schoolroom as we had when Miss Crawsby taught. We knew by now what to expect.

If we did wrong, we took the consequences. After the first term, we got to know him better and found him to be a good scout.

He would play baseball and football and would teach us what he knew about each. What he liked best was boxing and he was good. He taught the older boys many ways of self-defense. If any of the boys got into a fight, he would let them fight as long as they fought fair. Some of our parents didn't like this, especially the mothers. He told them that we couldn't injure each other seriously. What was a black eye or a bruised face but a sign of courage in a boy who would fight to defend himself or for what he thought was right?

I know, for I had to fight about every three days, and I would come home all bruised up. Father would ask where I got the bruises. I would tell him; "Fighting." He said; "If you have to fight, then fight; but you can't lick them all. If they know you will fight if necessary, you won't have to when they know they can't push you around." Well, I did do a lot of fighting, because there was a boy named Ed P. who would pick a fight with me about twice a week. He always licked me. If my sister saw us fighting, she would pull me out of the fight and stay with me so I couldn't fight. This was worse than getting licked, for the kids would yell at me that I was a quitter and afraid of getting a licking, which I would have got. Ed was the best fighter of the kids his size, and I was his size.

Ed would pick a fight knowing I wouldn't back down or run. He wouldn't pick a fight with John, for he had doubts about licking him. John tried to teach me but couldn't seem to help me. He asked why I didn't stop fighting with Ed. I told him the more I fought, the more I would learn, and some day I was going to lick Ed good.

THE HOME
ON THE AVENUE

We moved from the Skipper Billie place to the house on the Avenue. (I was seven going on eight years old at this time). We were close to Lock's Cove, in a section that was dubbed "Skunk Alley." (It was rightly named, for the skunks seemed to overrun the place.)

I had a wonderful time while we lived in this house, for I was older. There were pastures for us kids to roam over.

John would come up to the house and play, but if one of my sisters came out of the house he would leave, for he was awfully bashful. I often told him my sisters wouldn't bother him, but he would leave just the same if they came near. So I asked them if they would stay away from us and they did the best they could. There was lots of room around the house, and the kids liked to gather there. There was always something doing, for what one kid couldn't think of to do, the others could.

I lived there on the Avenue about eleven years of my life. I'll try to relate what happened during that time.

I was shown how to build a box trap. You could catch anything that could get into it. The first thing I caught was a cunny rabbit, and when I took it out of the trap, it cried so hard and loud I let it go. The next thing I caught was a crow. When I put my hand in to take it out, it picked (sic) my hand so hard it made it bleed, so I took the trap home and let it out in one of Father's chicken pens. I told one of the boys, named Accie, but he wouldn't believe me. I told him to come to the house and see for himself. When we got there, the crow wasn't in the pen, and to this day I don't think he believed I caught that crow. I found out my sister who owned (a) cat had let the crow out.

Mrs. Sargent gave me a wonderful squirrel cage. It had a treadmill wheel that would turn around so the squirrel could get exercise. The other part of the cage was made fancy and painted with gold trim. The prettiest thing a boy could have was what I thought, and that exercise wheel turned so easily. If you blew hard at the top, it would turn. Now I had to set the box trap where there were red squirrels. The second day I caught a squirrel and put him in the cage. The first thing he did was to go into the wheel; and didn't he spin it! It went so fast it looked as if the squirrel was running out in the open. He kept it up until he was exhausted and lay in the wheel, panting. I put food and water in the cage but he wouldn't eat. The next time I caught one was three days later. I put him in the cage. He also went first to the wheel and turned it fast until the other one came in it. The wheel was going so fast it pulled the feet from under the first squirrel so that he fell on his hind-end and rolled sideways. His weight stopped the wheel and both squirrels went into the house. They ate the food I gave them. I guess the first was so hungry, it started eating before the other one ate everything up.

I caught another squirrel and I don't know whether it was the last or one of the others. The other two didn't like it for they fought this one. The hair on parts of his body was off, his front left foot was cut and a third of his tail was bitten off. I finally let him go and the other two got along all right. I kept them until I was tired of them and then let them go too.

Admiralty Village was the land owned by a man called "Uncle" and it was the area where we roamed. There was pasture land, hay fields and woods, and we used to play there all the time. Philbricks Road, as they now call it, was Philbricks Lane when I was a kid. We would drive our cows where Uncle's cowyard was on Whipple Road. They would go to their pasture via the lane passing under the railroad bed by a culvert, and feed in the pasture which is Admiralty Village now.

Just as you entered the pasture on the left, Uncle had a big hay barn on the hill by the railroad track, and cut hay by the barn in the big hay field to the west.

Woodlawn Avenue was a dead end, and Grammy L. lived in the last house. We played baseball near Uncle's hay barn after he cut the hay. I would hide my glove and bat behind the barn so I could sneak off Sunday afternoons. All the other boys who could would be there too. We played there a number of summers. It was far enough out of sight of the houses around there that they were not disturbed by our noise, with the exception of two houses on Philbricks Lane and they didn't seem to mind. Playing games on Sundays was against the law, then.

One of the houses on Philbricks Lane became vacant and a man and his wife moved in. These houses were owned by Uncle. The wife was very religious and thought she was pretty good, but we knew different. She would lie and steal fruit and vegetables. She even hounded her husband until he didn't know he had a soul of his own.

Between Philbricks Lane and the Avenue were Uncle's woods, and in about the center was a hill. There were good-sized pine trees on the top of the hill, and between four on the very top we built a platform we called the "Lookout." It was a good view. We could see Portsmouth to the south; the harbor, ocean, and the Isle of Shoals to the east; and Spruce Creek to the north, besides a lot of streets and coves in the Back Channel, and the north side of the navy Yard. To the west was Roger's Woods which grew on a hill higher than our hill, so we couldn't see very far in that direction.

When the Portsmouth, Kittery and York electric road was being built, they used Lock's Cove to store lumber of all descriptions, even the pilings. Five long logs, held together on each end by a short chain with old horseshoes as staples to fasten the chains to the logs, were placed at the mouth of the Cove as a boom to keep the lumber in. When the tide was low, they all rested on the flats. When the things floated, we kids had lots of fun running from one piece of lumber to the other, as river drivers do on a log drive. Some pieces were big enough to support us but others wouldn't hold us. After the boom had been in the water a while, it got slimy and very slippery. The summer boarder who lived nearby would give us kids 2 cents if we could walk the length of one log, 4 cents for two logs, 6 cents for a third log, and 10 cents for four logs and 25 cents if we could walk all five logs. It was almost impossible because all the logs would roll. My best was three logs. We took some funny spills, and it took all sorts of comical body-twisting to keep our balance.

One night Zeek didn't get home for supper. He was about seven. We waited and waited but he didn't come. About nine o'clock that night, Father said to me, "Let's go and search for him." He didn't say where. We went to the barn and got a lantern each. It was then that Father said he thought Zeek must be drowned in the Cove, and that he had probably fallen between two pieces of timber which came together and that he couldn't separate. When we arrived at the Cove, Father said we would walk in a given direction about five feet apart and as far as the lumber would support our weight, because the tide was coming in. We hadn't been searching long before some of the people around the Cove asked us what we were doing. When we told them, they went home and came back with lanterns. In no time there were more than fifteen people searching. Before the incoming tide stopped the search, everyone agreed Zeek wasn't in the Cove. It was awful for me, for I expected to find him drowned any minute. Mother was beside herself with fear and Father said he would warm his buttocks when he got hold of him. The worst thing they thought of was that he might have fallen down a well. It was ten o'clock when they sent me to bed, for I was only eight and a half years old. It was a long while before I went to sleep, although I was very tired, and I missed him for we slept together. The next thing I knew Zeek was with Mother who was seeing he got in bed. When she was gone and he was in bed, I asked him where in the world he had been. He said to a dance down at Kittery Point. I was so sleepy I didn't ask any more questions. I knew I would find out in the morning. Having him in bed with me at that time was all I asked. What had happened was this: Zeek met George (the one who ran from the schoolroom the time of the fight) and asked where he was going all dressed up. George said to a dance down to the Point. Zeek wanted to go and said his sisters would be at the dance, for he had heard them say they were going. He asked one of the boys standing by to tell my Mother, and the boy said he would. Zeek rode off on the handle-bars of George's bicycle to the Point. We found out later the boy thought Mother would give him a scolding, and when he knew about everybody searching for Zeek, he got more frightened. Zeek didn't get home until twelve-thirty. Mother and Father, when they saw he was all safe at home, didn't give George a scolding or Zeek a licking, as he had promised.

A few years later, I got a wound on my leg playing hockey – I was kicked by another player's skate – about the middle and at the side of the shinbone. I bandaged it and put on a good healing salve, but no scab would form. It wasn't much of a cut and didn't bleed much, but it wouldn't heal. There was only a discharge that would wet the bandage. The leg pained me very little. One night after I had taken a bath, I was wiping my leg and the towel caught on something sticking out of the hole that wouldn't heal. I got hold of the piece that was sticking out and it moved. I could see it move under the skin down my leg for about an inch and a half. I called Mother's attention to it, and she told me to go to the doctor's office the next day. He looked at my leg and asked how long ago this had happened. I told him about two weeks. Then he took a sharp instrument and cut the hole larger, and drew out a sliver of bone about an inch and a half long. The doctor said I had good blood because the wound would have become infected if the blood had not been good. He also said that if he had seen it at the start, he could have bandaged the leg tightly so the sliver would be pressed back and have knitted with the shin-bone, but that it wouldn't knit with my using the leg muscles walking and playing without a tight bandage. Therefore, it was better to remove the sliver since it had been away from the shinbone as long as two weeks. It healed all right and never bothered me.

Fourth of July was a day that was the best of all the year. There was no restriction on what you could buy. You could buy the largest firecracker of all – it was an inch and a half in diameter and a foot long, and sold two for twenty-five cents. Only adults could buy them. The biggest one I could buy at my age was a half-inch by five inches long, and that would blow your hand off if you held it too long. Families would buy rockets, roman candles, pinwheels and such. From midnight the night before until the next night, there was no sleep unless you were so tired the noise couldn't bother you; and by nine o'clock Fourth of July night, there was practically no noise. Because the celebrations started after the stroke of twelve the night of the third, bonfires were lit at midnight and everything continued until noon and then tapered off to nothing about nine at night. Those twelve hours, especially the first six, there was a constant racket. On the night of the Fourth, by the time it was dark enough to set off fireworks again, eighty per cent of the people were in bed, for they had been up all the night before; and those who hadn't gone out to celebrate couldn't sleep for the noise. They, too, were in bed by nine-thirty July Fourth night.

We had a model of a field artillery cannon scaled a quarter smaller. The wheels were eighteen inches in diameter, the barrel sixteen inches long, the breech three-and-a-half inches in diameter, and the muzzle two inches with an inch-and-a-half bore. We would wheel the cannon all over town and we had to be careful how we pointed it, for the concussion from the blast would break windows at twenty feet. Father said he could spot us all over town by the blast of the cannon. It was louder than most explosions and had a different sound.

I have rambled from the subject of the Fourth of July. Coming back to the subject, one Fourth, when I was around ten years old, about nine o'clock in the morning of the Fourth, I was pouring cups of (gun) powder in a hole in the ground. I laid a fuse to each charge and then watched if go off. This made a quick flash and white smoke would curl up. It made no noise but was pretty. I had done this a number of times, but the next time I poured the powder in the hole and was leaning over, about to light the fuse, the powder went off too soon, burning my face and hands badly. To this day I don't know how it happened, unless a spark in the hole set it off. Yet you would think it would have exploded when I first poured the powder in. Mother sent for the doctor who bandaged up my eyes, and for three days and two nights I couldn't see anything. The doctor thought if my eyeballs were severely burned I would be blind. Of course, they didn't tell me. Every time I see a blind person he has my sympathy, for those three days and nights were a long time. I couldn't feed myself, and didn't know the time of day or where I was unless they told me when they moved me. The evening of the third day, the doctor removed the bandages and told me to look out of my right eye and tell him what I could see. I could see a lit candle and people around me, and I could see Mother. Then he asked me to look out of the left eye and to tell what I saw. I could see the same as I did with the right eye. Mother began to cry and I asked why. They told me. If my eyeballs had been burned badly and adhered to my eyelids, the eyeballs would have to be removed. Then I knew why they kept asking if my eye(s) hurt. They didn't, but my face, nose and cheeks did. My lips were the worst and the inside of my nose was burned. Having inside and outside burns was very painful. When my face healed and left no scars, I was very thankful.

Each spring, four of us boys would have a fish market at Charlie's house. There was a small shed that we used. The only fish we sold were flounders, for ten cents a dozen. We would take turns every two days. One would stay and clean fish, one would sell, and two would catch the fish. We fished from bridges and wharves. The lines we used had sinkers on one end. Up from the sinker about a foot was the first hook, further up the line again was another hook until there were four hooks on the line, each hook tied to the main line with a longer line than the previous hook. We did this so the hooks would be on or near the bottom, as the line slanted up from the sinker to where we stood. I never caught four at one time, but three often, and two quite frequently. Each of us used three lines, and if the fish were hitting well, we were kept busy. A good day's catch would be about two hundred fish. Some we threw back; we only kept fish eight inches or longer. We hauled our lines, bait and pails in two cars(boxes), and a hundred fish was quite a pull home, especially uphill. We fished in March and early April and kept the fish in the snow. What fish we didn't sell, Charlie's father used in his garden as fertilizer.

The next venture for earning was the paper route I bought from Joe K. This route was known as the Pine Hill and lower foreside route, and had about a hundred customers. I carried two bags and left one on Mr. Patch's porch at the depot. I then delivered from one bag up the Rodgers Road as far as the cemetery and back to Manson Avenue; then I cut through to the Hayes' house and to Whipple road and back to Mr. Patch's. I picked up the second bag and delivered from Williams Avenue to the waterfront, to Lock's Cove and then again on Whipple Road. Finally, on to Fred Bradbury's at the end of Ferry Lane. It took two hours and a half to make the delivery. But on Saturday night it took three hours or more because some people forgot it was pay-night; others didn't have any change, only bills, and they didn't want to break them. They said they would pay the next week. Only the next week, they would pay for the week before and not the week that was due. I learned a lot about people on this route. Some were kind and thoughtful, others tried to cheat me, and others were always growling about this and that—not at me, but at the world in general. I often thought of what they must get out of life.

The last house was Fred Bradbury's. He had a wholesale grocery store in

Dover, New Hampshire, and was quite a wealthy man. He kept servants who lived in a small house close to his big house. I liked him, for he would kid me or play jokes on anyone he could. One cold, rainy night in October, when I delivered his paper, a servant came to the door and I told her it was pay-night. She told Mr. Bradbury who came to the door and asked me in. I said I was all wet, but he grabbed me by the arm and hauled me into the kitchen entryway. He told me to take off my raincoat and rubber boots, for I was to stay for supper. I told him I had had my supper, but he knew I hadn't. He told me to hurry-up, for supper was ready and he was hungry. I was glad my stockings were clean and had no holes in them, for I had to sit in my stocking feet. He placed me beside his daughter Winifred, who was about a year older than I, and asked me all sorts of questions. When he asked me why my face was so red and told me Winifred wouldn't bite me, I wished I could have fallen through the floor. Being waited on by a servant, which I had never been before, and sitting beside the girl, I felt very much out of place. To this day I couldn't tell you what we had to eat. I was so glad when I got away, but you can bet Mr. Bradbury enjoyed that meal.

One of my sisters had a boyfriend we despised. He was the most conceited person I had ever known, and a bragger as well. They say he was an excellent drummer. I know he played the xylophone, for he would bring it with him and hammer away on it by the hour. Each time he was through playing a piece, he would wait for us to applaud. He was disgusting, but Sister seemed to like him, so Zeek and I took over. You see, he would wait at the front door until he could hear the electric car come up Austin School Hill. He would have just enough time to run down the Avenue to meet it. We stretched a rope across the yard from the chestnut tree to the currant bush at the corner of the house, about eight inches from the ground. Boy, what a flop he took. He couldn't stop to argue about it because if he did, he would miss the last trolley to Portsmouth. That would mean a three-mile walk home and he would be over his anger by the time he made his next call. It had to be a still night to hear the trolley come up the hill, and you can believe we knew the still nights. You would think he would know how we tripped him, for the tree and the bush were the only things in the yard we could tie a rope to, and he could have judged where the rope was and jumped over it. He was awfully dumb or lovesick!

During the Spanish-American War, after the Battle of Santiago when we defeated Admiral Cervera's fleet, the prisoners were brought to a stockade that was built on Seavey's Island (where the Naval Prison now stands). The stockade was built hurriedly and as cheaply as possible. The houses were built of plain, matched boards. The roofs were of smooth edged boards covered with tarpaper. In the spring of 1899, the stockade was sold to the highest bidder to be torn down and carried from the island. I was fourteen that year and had a boat of my own. One day, rowing by, I saw the pile of boards and tar- paper that were piled near the shore. I thought now easy it would be to take them away by boat. I talked this over with some of the boys and we decided to build a clubhouse in the back of our field in a clearing made by cutting the bushes away. When the tide was low boats couldn't be seen, for the shore was shaped at a sharp angle so the boats were not far from the piles of board and paper. We didn't bother with short boards but took the ones about fourteen feet long. We decided to make the clubhouse about 600 yards from (the) high-water mark in Lock's Cove. The boys who didn't go after the boards were to lug them to where we were going to build.

We agreed to build the clubhouse eighteen feet long by fourteen feet wide, six feet across the back and eight feet across the front. We had no idea of the amount of boards and tar paper we would need, so we got plenty of each, for the getting was good. The next question was where to get the two-by-fours for studding. These we found in the fence along the right-of-way of the York Harbor and Beach Railroad. We marked straight ones with a white rag tied to the bottom wire so when the first moonlight night came we could go get them. We had a hard time separating them from the posts. They were spiked on to hold. We wanted windows and a door, (so I) inquired around and swapped tarpaper and boards for them. We wanted nails to build with, so we went to the stockade and picked them up.

We completed the clubhouse in May the next year. We furnished the interior with chairs and pictures from members (what they could get from home). You should have seen the dishes, all sizes and colors, and the knives and forks were quite an assortment; but we kids didn't mind so long as they were useful. We had a grand time when we had the housewarming. Each boy asked his mother to cook something for the occasion.

Twelve of us boys belonged to the club and we had a great time at that dinner. We were halfway through the dinner when our mothers and neighbors came to call on us. They stepped just inside the door to watch us. Hattie was crippled, a hunchback. To our surprise and delight, two of the neighbors wheeled her to the club. When we saw her at the door, we lifted her chair in. We told her and the neighbors who had brought her that we would see she got home when she wanted to go. We then and there elected her "Mother of the Club." And darned if she didn't cry. One of the younger kids said she didn't have to be if she felt that bad about it. That made us all laugh.

We all knew where the key to the club was hidden and the last one out locked up. At the club we had books, games and cards for pleasure. For these games and cards we had rules that were agreed upon and were posted in the clubroom. There were no dues. If anyone wanted to cook and eat there, he could. When the sweet corn and tomatoes were ripe and the potatoes large enough, we had many good dinners from the neighbors' gardens. They would give us vegetables; we never stole from their gardens. We knew they raised them for their own use. If we asked for corn and they said they were going to can it, that was all right with us; but they would always find something they could spare, like tomatoes, shell beans or cucumbers.

When kids are growing up, they don't care for one thing long, so the club didn't last long. I used it more than any other kid, but it wasn't fun being the only one there. The boys called a meeting to quit the club for good. I asked them why they wanted to quit, and they said their parents didn't want them to go to the clubhouse because it was said we were playing poker for money and were stealing hens and vegetables and cooking and eating them at the club. We all knew this was a lie and we could guess who had told these things. Well, the vote was to quit. We drew lots for the things in the club and if one drew things he didn't want, he was to take them just the same or swap then with another, but it had to be taken from the club.

I sold the clubhouse to Cris R. for ten dollars. He moved it on the snow with skids under it for the short distance to his place. He used it for a workshop. There were twelve members when we build the club, but two had moved away, so I gave each boy a dollar and that was the last of the club.

When I was about eleven, Father said that I should learn to milk a cow. He said it was something that anyone could do, and I would try anything once. I learned to milk, to my sorrow, for afterwards Father wanted me to milk all the time. He said I ought to, for he worked all day and I had more time than he did.

Our next-door neighbor was an inquisitive woman. We didn't care much for her, but she had the best raspberry patch –large and juicy berries. It was hard to get into it by day. At night we found we were getting bugs in our mouths because we couldn't see. Stinkbugs ate the berries at night, and they were awful to get in your mouth. The woman could see the patch out of her kitchen windows and we couldn't crawl to it because it was out in the yard with nothing around it. We thought up a way to get in at the back of the patch, and if we didn't stand up, we wouldn't be seen. We would draw lots and the one who lost had to go to the side door and knock. He would ask her if she had any errands for him to do. While he was at the door, the others would sneak in and pick their hats full. When they wanted to come out they would crow like a crow, and he would go to the side door again, rap and run before she opened the door. I never saw her picking the berries and I knew most of them rotted on the vines. She never liked any of us, and if she knew anything mean about us she would make it her business to tell everybody who would listen.

The time I looked for a burglar was one night when I was reading, lying on the couch. About twelve-thirty I heard a noise. I listened and continued to read. Then I heard it again and it was a noise, all right. I thought someone was trying to get in the front door or parlor window. I sneaked up to Father's room and woke him and told him what I had heard and thought. He got up and each of us got a revolver. He said I was to go to the parlor by the dining-room door and he would go through by the front hallway.

He said to stay down and close to the floor, and not to stand up until we spoke to each other. I went on my hands and knees until I got to the parlor door, crept to one side and opened it as softly as I could. When it was opened, I lay on my stomach and waited for Father at the hall door to the parlor. It wasn't long before I saw it open, and I kept still to see if the burglar or Father had opened it. After a short time, I could see Father on the floor, so I spoke to him and we agreed there wasn't anybody in the room. When we heard the noise come from the cellar, we went down and found a skunk that had fallen in the cellar through an open window. It had fallen seven feet but it wasn't hurt that we could see. Fortunately, the cellar doorsill is about eight inches from the cellar floor. I could watch him while I opened the door. The next morning he was gone.

GRAMMY LOVE

Grammy Love lived alone in a small house at the end of the Avenue. She had no near neighbors, which seemed to please her. She was the quietest woman I have ever known.

When I first knew her, she was about eighty year old, did all her own housework and lived apart from all the other families around her. She had a son who lived about a mile away and he looked after her all he could. He sawed and split her wood or anything she wanted, but she wouldn't live with him –she said she would live her life the way she wanted to live; she was very independent and extremely shy and quiet. She would sit by her kitchen window where she could look up the Avenue and smoke her clay pipe. If anyone came, she would hide the pipe.

One day I came around the corner and caught her with the pipe in her mouth. I smiled at her. She took the pipe out and quietly smiled, and put the pipe back in her mouth again.

A short time later after this, she was in her backyard and had an ax stuck in a piece of wood. I took the ax from her, got it out and split the piece and some more pieces that were sawed. There weren't many pieces, and I carried the wood into the kitchen, filled the wood-box, and then split the small amount of sawed pieces left. I asked her when she'd like me to come around again and split some more pieces if Dick, her son, didn't come. She said, "Never mind," and went into the house and didn't even thank me for what I had done. They said she was a queer woman, and now I knew she was.

Two days later I went by and looked in

the yard, and there was no wood sawed or split. I asked her for the bucksaw, but she said she would saw some wood when she needed any. I told her I wanted the saw so she got it, and I sawed and split enough to last a couple of days. To my surprise, she thanked me and asked me if I would buy her some tobacco. She said she would write a note asking them to sell it to me, for I was too young to buy it. She also wanted me to call at her son's house and ask how he was, for she knew he must be sick. He was sick, and I told him I would look after Grammy until he got well. The tobacco she had me buy was Navy Black, the strongest pipe tobacco sold at that time.

During the time I worked for her, she never spoke to me except to thank me when I got through. One day when I was going by, she came to the door and called me by my first name (I was surprised, for I didn't know she knew my name), and asked if I would like some tea. "No," I said, as I didn't like tea. Then she said she had just baked some bread and asked if I would like to have some. I said, "Yes."

We went into the kitchen, and while I was eating I asked her if I could do anything for her. She said, "No." I tried talking to her, but she never made any reply, so I left; and I don't know to this day what she wanted. It might have been to give me the bread or that she wanted company, but she didn't talk to me and didn't ask me to stay when I left. She seemed a very distant woman. When her son got well he asked me what he owed me for helping his mother. I told him nothing, but he insisted I take $2.

It wasn't more than a year later when her son found her dead in bed in the morning. "Heart attack," they said. Mother and the neighbors went to the funeral, and all the relatives she had there were her son and his wife.

HATTIE

Hattie had a hunched back from a fall down a flight of stairs. Some days she could walk around, but mostly she had to use a wheelchair. She was the kindest and best-natured person I have ever known. Added to her trouble, her father had sores on both legs below the knees. He could not always do the work outside the house, so six of us boys in the neighborhood took it upon ourselves to help them out. We split the time up so two boys looked after them a week, which meant we had one week on and two weeks off. We would saw and split wood and, in fact, do all the outdoor work if the father wasn't able to work. We helped him plant and hoe his garden, and would harvest it for him if necessary. We would feed the hens, kill and pluck a chicken if they wanted one, see that they had coal from the cellar and empty the ashes. They had apple, pear and cherry trees in the front yard. We picked the fruit from all of them, especially the cherry trees, for they had the best cherries of any tree I knew about. Hattie asked us to pick and sell them for her. She wanted to give us half of what we made, but we would only accept a quarter.

You no doubt ask yourself why six boys would do this for them. One reason was that Hattie was so kind and cheerful, and her father did as much as he could and sometimes more that he should have. Another thing was that we always got something to eat from her. The first chocolate pudding I ever ate, she gave me. In the winter we always shoveled their snow. My father was good about this, for in the summer when it was my week to work for them, I didn't have to work in his garden.

We had helped them about two years when they got a boarder, a Marine named Louis. He was stationed at the Navy Yard barracks. I didn't think much of sailors and marines in those days and I told Hattie so. I liked him at our first meeting. He wasn't an ordinary Marine. He was a clerk for the major and didn't have to do guard duty, drill or march. Louis grew up in an orphanage. He was very well educated. He could do about everything: cook, sew, sweep, wash, iron and a lot of work outdoors too. We six boys weren't needed after he came, but we would always stop by to see if she wanted us to do anything. She married Louis after three years, and he left the Marine Corps and worked in the Navy Yard as a clerk in the Supply Department. Her father died soon after they were married and they took in Hattie's Uncle Billie, who was an old man partly blind. He worked outdoors doing what he could, but didn't live long after he came, so Hattie and Louis were alone. Hattie didn't survive her Uncle long, and the house couldn't hold all who came to her funeral.

THE MEN

I want to tell you about (some) men who were very good to me. I thought a lot of them and I know they thought a lot of me.

First, there was Ed. B. He lived next door and was a carpenter and boat-builder by trade. He fished for lobsters as a sideline before and after his workday and on Saturdays and Sundays. He made his own lobster pots and tarred the twine as well. Twine is used to knit the heads in the pots. It was a sticky, messy job handling that cold tarred twine. We used lard on our hands so they wouldn't stick to the twine, and if you got the tar on your clothes, it was very hard to get off. We used old stockings to protect our arms. The tar would get under our fingernails and Mother used to scold me for having such dirty-looking nails.

I not only liked to knit the heads but also liked the stories he would tell while we worked. Some were true and some very false, for he was a great storyteller. His stories about the fishing he did on schooners out of Gloucester on the Grand Banks were very interesting.

My (own) motorboat was anchored off Lock Cove entrance. I had my wherry to row to it, and one day my oars were missing. I borrowed a pair until I could buy a new pair for myself. When I got them, I put a hole in the handle lengthwise to the oar and wrote on two pieces of paper that these oars belonged to me. I put the papers in the hole in each oar and then plugged the holes and smoothed them over so they didn't show. Near the end of each blade, I scratched a mark that I could tell them by and painted them a color that I mixed myself, a color no one could duplicate. In about two weeks they were gone. I had an idea who had them, so I started to search around his shed and buildings. At last I found them under the back porch, way in back, partly covered with leaves. I crawled under and got them and just as I was leaving, he saw me. I ran and he ran after me. It was a short distance to the wharf and I got there first. The owner of the wharf and Ed B. were there, and they wanted to know what the trouble was. I said I had found my oars under the fellow's back porch. (We called this fellow "Gosh Edgar" for he was always saying "gosh" and his first name was Edgar.) He said they were his oars, so I asked him why they had been way back under his porch, partly covered with leaves. He said they were on his property and I took them and that was stealing. I said I could prove that they belonged to me if he would just wait a minute. I told the owner of the wharf to take his knife and remove the plug at the end of each oar. I also showed the scratches I had made. Ed became interested, and when Gosh

Edgar stared to leave, he grabbed him by the shoulder. Anyone held by his big strong hand didn't go far. When the plug was removed and the paper taken out and read, Ed turned him around facing the end of the wharf, took him by the neck and seat of the pants, ran him to the end and threw him in the river. The tide was half up and he had a drop of ten feet or more so he hit the water hard. While he was swimming to shore, he said Ed had spoiled his watch and clothes. Ed said he would spoil more than that if he ever took anything from me again, and the owner told him to stay off his property in the future.

I would like to tell you of another Ed, Ed K. He seemed to like me even when I was a small kid. When I was playing with his nephew he would stop and talk and ask questions, and our friendship grew with the years.

My first job after high school was working for Ed K. He owned a meat, provision and fish store. I worked in the store and drove the delivery team. William Dean Howells was one of our customers. When I delivered at his home, he always talked with me a lot and asked me all kinds of question. I think he liked me.

Another customer was Captain Shackfork, a retired trans-Atlantic liner captain. He had plenty of money, and his wife and old-maid daughter were very high-hat. The market had to carry them on credit for a month's supplies, but we charged them about four per cent more, the rate the banks charged. One time when I presented his month's bill, he asked his daughter to go to his room and get his purse. He talked to me while we waited. After a while, his daughter called and said she could not find his purse. He said that he knew G--d--- well she couldn't find it, that he would have to find it himself. When I left, I thought that they weren't any different from any other family, and were just show-offs with their high-hat ways.

My third special friend was Frank T. I first met him when I was about eight years old.

It was a cold winter day, and as I was passing his shop, I saw smoke coming from the chimney and I heard him pounding inside. I knocked on the door and he shouted, "Come in." He asked me what I wanted. I answered that I wished to get warm. I knew he had a fire by the chimney smoke, and I knew he was in because I could hear him pounding. He laughed and said, "Stay as long as you like." I liked the way he laughed and the way he asked me questions. He was building a boat, and I guess I asked a lot of questions myself.

He was a typical New England Yankee, and so was his wife. They owned an extra-large house and kept summer boarders. The arrangement was ideal. The boarders were the ones who made sure the house was filled during the summer. They formed a committee and brought the people they wished to the house. Most of them came from Malden, Massachusetts. They were like a very large family.

Mrs. T. looked out for the meals and the hired help, who did all the work. Mrs. T. also supervised and furnished the supplies. She asked the boarders what they liked and disliked, and it was said that she set a wonderful meal. Mrs. T. didn't know how long a boarder was going to stay. That was for the committee to know. No doubt she and the committee asked each other questions. Everything seemed to run smoothly, and all had a good vacation.

Frank's duties were outdoors. The boats he built he would rent or sell. He also looked after them when the season was over. He would store them in winter and paint them in the spring, if necessary, for a price. If the boarders wanted to fish, he would tell them what bait to use and see they had the proper equipment. He also told them where to go at the time of tide to fish.

Between the house and wharf, on the flat of land just before it sloped to the shore end of the wharf, he build what they called the summer house. It was quite a large building. There were four hammocks swung in the center. The sides and ends were open with settees along both sides and the end opposite the shore. The women used them in the daytime and the men evenings.

I wish I could go there again and listen to the stories those men told about their experiences. Some among this group were men who held or had held high positions. Two were retired captains of transatlantic ocean liners; three were bankers; two were lawyers; and the rest were businessmen. They didn't mind if some of the natives joined them, for most of then listened and didn't enter the conversation, unless asked.

In the fall after the boarders had left and on through the winter and spring, I was at Frank's. He was always working in his shop either for others or for himself. I liked his boat building best. One day when he was drilling from the outside through planking and rib, he missed the rib and swore. I told him I could get inside the boat and drill from the inside out, and I could drill the center of the ribs and the right distance into the plank, for I was small and could move around better inside the boat. We tried it and it worked perfectly. He was pleased, for we could rivet a boat and save a third of the time over the old way. I wasn't always (working) with him, but when he was ready to rivet up a boat he would tell me this was a two-person job. We would agree on a time and I would stay until the boat was riveted. He wanted to pay me but I said no; I didn't have much to do and enjoyed working with him. But at Christmas he mailed me a ten-dollar bill. I took it back to him and asked him to take it, for I didn't think I had earned that much. He said he wanted me to keep it, for what I had done for him was worth more than ten dollars; and besides, he liked to have me around when he was at work.

Frank T. was a man well-liked by all who knew him.

THE RIVER

The river was the most profitable and enjoyable place for me. From the time I was eight to the age of manhood, I enjoyed the river.

First, when very young, I fished from the wharves and bridges. At nine I could swim and dive. I never was afraid of the water; I've fallen in many times and every time was startled but never afraid.

When my chum John was ten years old, his father allowed him to use his small dory. I was nine and my father knew I could swim and allowed me to go with him. We had a wonderful time, and made money as well. The dory was about fourteen feet long and two could row it. With both of us rowing, we could go anywhere we wished.

First we picked winkles (which are saltwater snails). They were used for bait by the Gloucester fishermen. We sold them for twenty-five cents a peck and we could pick about a bushel from the last quarter of the ebb to the first quarter of the flood tide.

John's father was a trawl fisherman and gave us his old trawls. The dictionary states that a trawl is a net, but to the fisherman, it is a long line with hooks tied to it with smaller lines about two feet long and tied to the line about every six feet. It is wound around the inside of a tub made of a half- barrel, and all the hooks are baited and laid on top of each other at a certain place. When the tub is turned upside down on a float surface and the hooks are toward the stern, the line will go into the water without snarling. When you set a trawl, you tie an anchor to one end of it with a line and buoy attached, and then row or let the tide carry you. The trawl enters the water and sinks to the bottom. If you were to use two tubs, you would tie the ends of the trawls together and tie another anchor and buoy to the end. Two trawls would be about 900 yards long.

What edible fish we caught were sold. The other we sold, too, for lobster bait at twenty-five cents a bushel. What we did was haul the trawl over the dory, take the fish off, rebait the hooks, and then let it in the water again. This is what we did when we left the schoolroom where Miss Crawsby taught, as I mentioned before. If we had the whole day, we could fish the trawl at slack tide and then anchor the dory where we thought we could catch fish by handlining –fishing with one line in hand.

Codfish would come in the river from about the middle of April until the end of May. We always fished for them and did quite well. Once we were anchored close by the black buoy at the mouth of the Channel and the fish were biting well. We had caught quite a few large cod when John caught something he couldn't hold, so I hauled in my line and helped him.

Well, the two of us couldn't handle it, so we wound the line around the tholepin and let the fish tire itself out. We had no idea what was hooked but we knew it was big. I guessed it might be a skate. We started to haul again, and we could get in the line, but when the fish was about eight feet from the boat, it dived and we couldn't stop it. We kept hauling until we got it beside the boat. I hooked it with the gaff and nearly went overboard. John tied a line to the gaff and we towed it to shore. It was a codfish and we took it to Gus' wharf. He was home and he weighed it. It weighed seventy-six pounds and eleven ounces. Gus, who had fished the Grand Banks, said it was next to the largest cod he had ever seen.

When the cod left the river, we fished for cunners, as we called them. They are a saltwater perch. We could sell them for ten cents a dozen, all cleaned. They were good to fry or to use in chowders. We had three or four eel pots set and could catch all we wished, but they didn't sell so well as other fish and were a messy job to clean. Lobsters we could get in plenty. At extreme low tide we could hook them from holes in the river bank around Fishing Island. Back of the Island at low tide, we would walk the flats covered with eelgrass and prod every hump we saw with a stick. Sometimes it was a rock, and sometimes a crab or a lobster. We had ten lobster nets made of a steel barrel hoop with netting tied to close the hole. We baited these with gropies or flounder with a hauling rig attached to the hoop the right way. We could catch a half-bushel at night in about two hours. Lobsters sold six of a quarter, boiled and delivered. I ate so many of them when we had the clubhouse and on outings that I don't care to eat them now.

I have (used) more lobster for tolling bait than I have ever eaten. This tolling bait was used to keep mackerel near the boat while fishing. This was great sport, for we used a mackerel jug that didn't require any bait. We used three lines, and if they were biting and it was a large school, we caught a lot. The people around this vicinity knew all about mackerel. You couldn't sell them a two-pound fish. The smaller the better, for the small fish were not so fatty and oily as the larger ones. Tinker and tholepin sold the best. Tinker were from nine to eleven inches long. Tholepins were from six to nine inches.

When the trolley line was being built, schooners brought in pilings, timbers, sleepers, etc. We kids loved to climb all over the shops and dive from crosstrees and bowsprits. I didn't have the courage to dive from the crosstrees, for they were half the width of the ship and seemed a long distance up.

We would spear flounder and gropies with a long slender pole with a steel barb at the end. On a calm day when the tide was low, we would push the boat along the bank with the pole and spear the fish. We called it "jabbing flounders.' You had to stand up in the stern or bow where you could see the bottom well. One day I saw a catfish about three feet long. I intended to spear it in the head but struck its back without hitting the back bone. That fish yanked me overboard and swan off with the pole.

There was (a) place in the Navy Yard that paid off well for the time we worked, and that was the Yard dump. About everything was dumped there except metals, which could be melted down. We were allowed to pile the things we thought people would buy on Frank's shore. He said that it must be kept neat at all times though. We put up a post and hung on it a locked box with a slot in it big enough for a silver dollar. Then we nailed up a sign saying, "If you see what you want, put in the box what you think it is worth, and please think hard." Sometimes we would find a note saying what someone had taken and that he would pay later. You would be surprised at the number of things we collected. Boiler tubes, two to four inches in diameter, sold well and were used for posts under small buildings and back porches. Old canvas went well, as did large pans, pots, bowls, pitchers, big ladles, tubs and broken butcher knives, if broken off at the end of the blade. Once we found a hawser four inches in diameter made of rawhide. We cut it up in five-foot lengths with a saw. It was very hard work.

This sold well and could be used for reseating chairs or tying up trees and shrubbery as it was soft and wouldn't chafe.

When my father gave me the wherry the spring I was eleven years old, I was a happy kid. The sail was almost new, but when I took the boat out I didn't think it sailed as well as other boats I had sailed. I told Frank I was disappointed in the way it fell off the wind when close-hauled. He said that it wouldn't sail well until a centerboard was put in, and he would help me build one. I had no idea where its proper place in the boat was, so he showed me. He said that it should be three-quarters the length of the boom and he measured from mast aft to the required length. We cut a slot an inch wide along twenty-eight inches of the center line fore and aft, or one-sixth the length of the boat. When we completed the work and put the boat back in the water, it sailed perfectly. We made a bowsprit and I had a jib made. Now I had a boat that was just right for river and harbor use. We quit John's dory and used my boat entirely. We rowed and sailed many miles in it.

The second spring I had my boat, John told me that his aunt had died. I told him I was sorry to hear it and asked him if he was fond of her. He said that he had seen her only twice, so I didn't feel too bad for him. John wasn't himself the next two weeks, and the third week, he hold me that he was going to move away. He said that his uncle owned a large dairy farm in Montgomery, Vermont, and he had asked John's mother and father to come help him on the farm. He had given them a guarantee of twice the money his father could make fishing. Now I knew what was making John act the way he was, and I wasn't quite myself after he told me either. John didn't want to live on a farm, for he had been around the saltwater all his life and didn't like going inland. I didn't like to have him go.

His father sold all their belongings he could, and John asked me to come down to the shore where he lived and he would give me the fishing gear that he couldn't sell. I went to his shore as he asked and he gave me two tubs of almost new trawl, some oars, fishing lines and a lot of new hooks. We put them in the boat, and when it was time for me to leave I said, "Thanks." John said, "You're welcome." I got into my boat and he climbed the bank going up to his house. He didn't look back once; and I am not ashamed to say that when I was out of sight, I cried. John and I were the very best of friends. He liked what I liked and I liked what he liked. He was the only chum I ever had, and after he moved to Vermont, I never heard from him again. How I missed him.

I tried to fish with the two lengths of trawl John and I had. But I alone could not get enough bait to keep them filled, so I decided to use only one. Nobody knows how lonesome it was. When I pulled the trawls the first time alone, I went ashore on Jamaica Island nearby and cried my heart out, it seemed. My mother knew how I felt and tried to help me by saying that everyone must part with someone he loves at some time, because life is like that.

Frank said to me one day, "The cod have left the river by now. What do you earn in an average day of fishing?" I told him that I got about a dollar a day. Then he said, "Why don't you take the trawls in and work for me awhile?" He said that he had three families to move and a lot of other work. He knew how sad I felt, and he wanted to get me off the river for a while. I was glad to accept his offer, for I needed company. But every time I saw my boat on the shore, a lump would come into my throat; but by working at a different job, the loneliness wore away a lot in time.

When John left (that) spring, I cleaned up the space that Frank had let us use to store the things for the dump. There wasn't much left, just some pipe and heavy canvas. I never went back to the dump or fished with the trawl for long after that, because these were the two things John and I liked to do best. With him gone, they gave me no pleasure, only heartaches.

When the mackerel came I stared to fish again. I was going up to the Navy Yard bridge to catch mackerel one morning at low tide when I saw that some fish had been left stranded in the eelgrass on Tripp's Cove. I thought they were herring…but when I got there I found they were mackerel. I had two pails in the boat and so I started to pick them up just as fast as I could to get all I could before the tide floated them out. I put them into the two pails and dumped them into the boat until I thought my back would break. I rowed back to where I kept my boat and partly filled it with water so I could wash the fish, for they were a little muddy. I put all the fish that I could in one barrel and tried to put the barrel in the boat. I couldn't so I had to take some fish out. I piled these on the shore close to the boat and then I put the barrel into the boat and filled it full. I put the fish from the shore in a second barrel and put it in the boat too. I covered the barrels with wet burlap bags. I then rowed to Portsmouth and landed at the floating stage at Cerres Street. A short distance away on Market Street was Down's Fish Market. I went in and asked Mr. Downs if he would buy the mackerel. He looked at them and said that he would send two of his men to take them to the fish market. The men came and I went back to the store with them. They placed each barrel on the scales, weighted it, dumped the fish in a bin and then weighted the barrel to get the exact weight of the fish. Mr. Downs took the paper with weight of the fish marked on it and he asked me to come into his office. He showed me the list price per pound of mackerel that size and multiplied it by the weight of the fish. I shall never forget those figures. It came to $7.76. "Gosh!" was all I said. He asked me what I had thought I would get and I said I thought around three dollars. He said he thought I had no idea how much they were worth and that is why he had shown me the list price so I would know he had not cheated me. I told him he had treated me wonderfully and thanked him.

I was fishing for cunners in an eddy at the back of the point on Jamaica Island, when I heard Mel S. taking to someone. It was a very calm day. Mel's dory had gone adrift and landed on Shackford's Point, about two hundred feet from where Mel's schooner was anchored. Shackford's daughter, an old maid, was reading a book under a spruce tree there. Mel was pleading with her to row his dory out to him. He asked her four times, but she made no reply. So Mel stripped to his birthday suit and swam to where the dory was, walked up the beach, got in his dory and rowed back to his schooner. Miss Shackford kept on reading and, no doubt, didn't even take her eyes from the book she was reading.

The next summer I was at the age when kids are extremely restless. I couldn't stick to doing anything long. Nothing seemed to please me long (adolescent period they call it now.) In those days they called us pests and said, "For goodness sakes, go do something and get out of my way."

I remember the day that I was catching mackerel about ten inches long and the boat was tied to the Navy Yard bridge. I was very busy fishing when something small hit me in the back. I turned around quickly to swear at whoever had done it. I know I had my mouth open to shout but no words came out, for the one who threw the pebble was the prettiest girl I had ever seen. She asked me what I was catching in the river. She had the sweetest voice I had heard. I told her and asked her if she would like to catch some too, and she said that she would like to try it. I tied a clean bag on her for an apron and told her how to fish. She did quite well and would have done better if I had spent more time instructing rather than admiring her. When the fish stopped biting, I rowed to shore and we sat in the boat, talking. I asked her if she had ever eaten mackerel and she said, "No, (Vermont) where I come from, freshwater fish is the only fish they have." I cleaned some for her to take home and told her to tell her mother to fry them in cornmeal with a little salt. I asked her if she would like to go fishing with me the next day and she said that she didn't know. She would like to go but she would have to ask her parents. To my delight, she was there on the shore waiting the next morning, and she had on sensible clothes and a rubber apron. We caught quite a few fish. She had a nice-sounding laugh and the cutest giggle I have ever heard. Oh, she was wonderful. Then I asked her if I could call at her house that night about seven o'clock so that I could meet her mother. She said, "Yes, do come tonight." I did, and they were fine people and were very nice to me. I told her all about myself and how John had to go to Vermont and how sad it had been for me, and how her coming from Vermont sort of healed the wound. She said that she was glad if she could help me in any way. You no doubt would call it puppy love, but whatever you say, I felt wonderful. I loved to talk to her and watch her lovely brown eyes. All at once, she put her hand on mine and asked if I would teach her to sail. After I got over the thrill of her hand, I said, "I would be pleased to teach you," and I did. Gosh! I would have done anything for her. After a short time she could sail the boat as well as I could. She loved it so well that she sailed most of the time.

We were together a lot, and you can bet I didn't use profane language or chew tobacco while I was with her. She sang in the church choir and had a nice soprano voice. She would sing at churches and entertainments and I would take her to the places. One day, she said that her parents had forbidden her to see me anymore. I asked why, and she said that one of the members of the church where she sang had told them all about me and that I wasn't a fit person for her to be with. I asked her to ask her mother if I could talk to her. She said that she would. When I talked to her mother, I told her that I wasn't perfect, but I wasn't as bad as that woman had told her I was; for I know who had talked about me, and it was more to get even with me than it was the truth. I asked her if she would read sealed letters from people who knew me, if I got them. She said that she would, so I did. When she had read them, she said that she was sorry, that she should have inquired around before taking the word of this woman. After that I thought more of my girl friend than ever. We were young lovers until her cousin introduced a friend of his to her–a young navy man—and off she went with him. I was so hurt I stayed at home and read books all winter.

In the fall, I entered high school and

from here on, my life entered a new stage.

There were a lot of boys and girls in school I had never met before so I got over feeling jilted. But I never cared for any particular girl. I went with the ones I liked best but never steady with any. I learned to dance and I hired a woman to teach me etiquette. I was very particular about how I dressed and I went to all the dances. There I met a lot of girls. I enjoyed dancing and the parties very much.

My parent moved from the Avenue to Roger's Road, which was a good distance from the river, so I sold my motorboat and gave the wherry to a kid who loved the river as I did when young. He was eleven, about the age that I was when I had the boat.

When I first lived on Roger's Road, I was eighteen, an apprentice on the navy Yard, and earning enough money to spend taking girls to dances and theaters. I started to play pool and bowl but wasn't good at either of them, so I quit. I always liked hunting, after moving away from the river, that was my major pastime.

I didn't go steady with any one girl. I

couldn't seem to find one that I liked better than the others, so I went out with a lot of them. I would take them home now and then, and I guess my grandmother, mother's mother, got disgusted with me, for she told me once, "You will go through the wood and pick a crooked stick." I told her that I wouldn't, for the more I went through the woods, the better I could judge good timber. I was having too good a time.

Although there were plenty of saloons in Portsmouth, I never drank very much, for I was disgusted with the way some of my friends spent their nights. I much preferred to go to a good show or a dance, or to stay at home and read a good book.

Eventually, I was courting a girl in Portsmouth and one in Dover. I would see each at least twice a week. One was a schoolteacher in Portsmouth, and the other a private secretary to the manager of the Pacific Printing Company. Both were very smart girls. Every chance (grandmother) got, she would tell me what a wonderful girl she thought the schoolteacher was. I also knew that the secretary was too occupied with her mother—so I married the schoolteacher, (lived in Portsmouth), and I had a very happy life.

Dear Readers, if you have stayed to the end of my story, I thank you. No doubt, you can think back on your life as you lived it and think of pleasant as well as unpleasant things, as I have done.

Good-bye –

THE KITTERY KID